Big Sky Mountain

The Beach Otters

ALEX MILWAY

Piccadilly
PRESS

First published in Great Britain in 2022 by
PICCADILLY PRESS
4th Floor, Victoria House, Bloomsbury Square, London WC1B 4DA
Owned by Bonnier Books
Sveavägen 56, Stockholm, Sweden
www.piccadillypress.co.uk

A CIP catalogue record for this book is available from the British Library.
ISBN: 978-1-84812-974-0
Also available as an ebook and audio
1

Printed and bound in China

Piccadilly Press is an imprint of Bonnier Books UK
www.bonnierbooks.co.uk

For Arnie

1

The Flare

Rosa was fiddling with a small broken radio out on the shore of Jewel Lake. The case had cracked long ago, and wires stuck out like unwanted hairs on an old woman's chin.

'Get stuck in!' said Grandma Nan, who was busy attending to Albert the Moose's antlers. He'd got them tangled up in vines, and he was getting very irate. 'I

can't wait to hear my favourite show
again after all these years!'

Rosa poked around, but no
sound came from the machine.

'I have no idea what I'm doing!'
she grumbled, threading a wire into a
little hole. A short 'FZZZZT!' burst out of
the tiny speaker, then it fell silent again.

'Ah, no one knows anything when they
start out,' said Nan. 'But you'll soon learn!'

Rosa puffed out her cheeks and tried
again, but her attention was stolen by a
glowing red star, that was rising up into
the clear sky, miles away in the distance.

It reminded her of a slow-moving
firework, drifting out over the
mountain.

'Nan!' she cried.

'What's that?'

Little Pig, the pygmy owl who kept watch over their home, flew out from his hiding place in the cabin's wall and up into the air.

'WARNING! WARNING!' he screeched, before swooping down to land on Rosa's head.

Nan wandered over with her hands on her hips, gazing at the sky. She took out her telescope and stretched it out to its full length.

3

'Well, blow my trumpet,' said Nan. 'That's a distress flare!'

'Is someone in trouble?' asked Rosa.

Nan scratched her head, already planning a course of action.

'It's been fired from out on the coast,' she said, tucking away her telescope. 'Right, then. We'll need at least a week's worth of supplies, and our sleeping bags.'

Rosa felt a swell of excitement within her.

'Are we going to the seaside?' she asked.

'Nothing else for it,' said Nan. 'If someone's in trouble, we've got to go and help them!'

Then Stick, the young wolf cub, came racing along the beach, full of joy and

excitement. She stopped and howled at
the sight of Rosa, then bounced over to
her.

'We're off to see the sea!' said Rosa,
scruffling Stick's fur from head to paw.

'I don't think so. Stick will have to
stay here,' said Nan, who was already

returning to the cabin to sort out her things. 'It's a very long way for those little legs.'

Rosa's heart sank.

'But look at her!' said Rosa. 'She's desperate to come.'

It was true – Stick was very keen. She was running circles around Rosa's legs.

'We don't know what awaits us out there,' said Nan, with authority. 'There could be all sorts of trouble. Besides, Little Pig can keep an eye on her.'

The owl was deeply unimpressed.

'ME!?' he screeched, flying up to perch on the roof of the cabin. 'No! No! No! No! No!'

'Albert will do it, then,' said Nan. 'He's a responsible animal.'

Albert had wandered over to the shore and was drinking from the lake. Rosa found it hard to believe he was that responsible.

'Are you absolutely sure?' pleaded Rosa.

'Absolutely, one hundred per cent,' said Nan. She walked into the cabin and closed the door.

'I'm sorry, Stick,' said Rosa, with a sigh. 'You have to stay behind.'

The little wolf ran away with a whimper and darted inside the cabin using the wolf-flap built into the wall of Rosa's bedroom. Stick came and went as she pleased, but she never strayed far from the cabin. They'd become firm, inseparable friends, and Rosa would find it hard to leave her behind.

7

Feeling a little dejected, Rosa joined Nan and helped pack their bags. She was getting used to their expeditions now, and they made an efficient team.

'It's a long journey,' said Nan. 'Up Gold River, over the foothills to Prickly Plain, and then down into Toe-Dipper Bay. It'll take two days at least.'

'Are we taking Florence?' asked Rosa.

Paddling Nan's canoe was one of Rosa's favourite things to do on Big Sky Mountain, and she took to the water every day to grow stronger and more experienced at it.

'Of course. The faster we can travel the better!' replied Nan, rolling up a blanket and stuffing it in her backpack. 'But most of the journey will be on foot.

Luckily for us, it's a beautiful one.'

Rosa collected tins of beans and dried food from their cupboards, attempting to plan ahead. She totted up the number of meals for each day on her fingers.

'We could be gone for a week,' said Nan. 'Don't hold back!'

Rosa's bag got heavier and heavier, and with each extra addition she tested the weight on her back. When she felt it was just about as much as she could carry, she fastened the drawstring at the top.

'Ready!' said Rosa.

'For all weathers!' said Nan, collecting their raincoats. 'OH!'

Nan stopped dead in her tracks.

'Swimmers!' she cried, with a clap of her hands.

'What are swimmers?' asked Rosa.

'To wear in the sea,' said Nan. 'I never pass up a dip in the sea.'

'But I don't have any,' said Rosa.

Nan opened a drawer and pulled out an ageing brown swimsuit that hadn't seen the light of day in years. She then dug around a little more and pulled out an even older one that carried a few moth holes.

'You can wear this,' said Nan.

Rosa was unimpressed. But she wasn't going to pass up a chance to swim in the sea.

'If you think it'll fit,' said Rosa.

Nan tied some large knots in the shoulder straps.

'Now it will,' she said. 'Perfect!'

She threw it to
Rosa, who slipped
it into her bag,
then they both
left the cabin.

'Look after
the cabin and
Stick for us,
Albert,' said
Nan, as she
dragged Florence to
the water's edge.

'I shall try,' grumbled Albert. 'And
when you return, perhaps you might
bring apples?'

'If we find any,' said Rosa, 'we will.'

'Life's not the same without apples,' he
said, sadly. He rubbed his antlers against

the gravelly ground, and wandered along
to munch on a tuft of grass.

'I wonder what we will find out there?'
said Rosa, stepping into the canoe.

'One thing for certain,' said Nan.
'Another adventure!'

2

The Sneaky So-and-So

Rosa and Grandma Nan left the canoe on the riverbank. They travelled through the low hills until they reached Prickly Plain, where a huge expanse of flowing grasses and wildflowers stretched out across the whole horizon, as far as the eye could see.

With the afternoon sun high overhead, Grandma Nan cut a speedy path through

the shimmering grass. Rosa did her best
to keep up, but her backpack seemed
to grow heavier by the minute, and she
wondered whether she'd packed one
too many tins of beans. Even so, a more
pressing concern were the millions of
insects buzzing around her. She quickly
realised it was best to keep her mouth
shut for fear of inhaling them.

'We can rest soon!' said Nan, noticing
that Rosa was slowing. 'If you look over
there, you'll see our home for the night.'

In the distance, a rocky outcrop of
granite erupted from the plain. It was the
only feature for miles and miles.

'It looks like a dog!' said Rosa,
noticing how the rocks rose up into an
animal-like shape.

'That's why it's called Wolf Tor,' said Nan. 'A tor is a high, rocky hill. There's plenty of shade and shelter for us there, and we'll get a good view of the land from the top. We can head on to the coast tomorrow.'

With the sun's heat beating down on them, they crossed the plain, eventually reaching Wolf Tor and a delicious slice of shadow. Rosa and Nan clambered up the dark grey boulders and sloping ground to the top of the tor. Little nooks and crannies abounded, and Rosa thought it would have made an excellent spot for a fort.

From the top of the tor, Rosa had a view in every direction. Big Sky Mountain towered up to the west, and

Jewel Lake and their cabin were hidden
somewhere out there, in amongst the
foothills. So too was Stick. Rosa couldn't
help worry about her, and she had to
hope that Albert was doing his best to
care for her.

But Rosa struggled not to feel excited.
Behind them, just on the top of the

horizon, she was almost certain she could see a thin blue line of sea.

'Is that the sea?' she said.

'It is indeed,' said Nan.

'I can't remember the last time I saw it,' said Rosa.

'It's been a while for me, as well,' said Nan. 'But Toe-Dipper Bay is worth the wait. I promise.'

Nan passed Rosa a water flask, and she glugged it down.

'Right, then,' said Nan. 'Let's eat.'

They started a small fire in a ring of stones and placed open tins of beans at its edge. The beans warmed slowly and Rosa gave them the occasional stir to stop them burning.

Once they'd eaten, they laid out their

sleeping bags and nestled down for the night. Without the fire it would have been pitch black, as the clouds had rolled in and blocked all of the moonlight. The swaying grass beneath the tor shushed and swished, night birds shrieked and hollered, but perhaps the loudest, scariest noise was Grandma Nan's snoring.

Rosa tried nudging her gran to put a stop to it, but Nan turned to iron when she slept and was impossible to move. Rosa couldn't sleep, and so she stood up, gazing out into the darkness. She struggled to make out anything in the gloom and found this unsettling, so she breathed deeply and tried to calm herself. And then she saw movement at the base of the tor.

With a shiver and a gulp, Rosa ducked down to hide. She gripped Nan's foot – fully covered in its sleeping bag – and shook it as hard as she could. Nan rolled over, oblivious, but at least she stopped snoring. Rosa had to be brave – she had to do this on her own.

She stood up again and peered down the slope, but she couldn't see anything out of the ordinary. Maybe she'd imagined it? Rosa placed another few branches on the fire and tucked herself back into her sleeping bag. But there was no way she could sleep. Her heart continued to beat heavily in her chest, and her eyes were wide open, scouring the rocks around them.

A few minutes passed, and Rosa's fear slipped away. Without noticing it, her eyes started to close. But just as she was falling asleep, a soft, wet tongue licked her face from chin to forehead.

Rosa screamed and leapt up. Her sleeping bag trapped her legs and she fell face first on to Grandma Nan, who also screamed – although in a more gruff, angry sort of way. Nan leapt up to defend herself, only to fall flat on her face on the ground as her legs, too, were stuck in a sleeping bag. They squirmed about in a bundle of arms and legs and blankets, and there at their heads was a little wolf.

'Stick!' cried Rosa, as the wolf licked
her again.

'What on earth?!' said Nan. She patted
the ground and found her glasses.

Stick howled joyfully as Rosa's racing
heart slowed.

'How did you find us?' asked Rosa.
'We've come so far!'

Stick sniffed the air to show that she'd
followed their scent all the way.

'Clever girl!' said Rosa.

'Silly animal, more like!' said Nan, crossing her arms. 'This is dangerous! We don't know what we might find.'

Stick didn't like being told off. She nuzzled herself into Rosa's sleeping bag to hide from Nan and her angry words.

'It's not the end of the world,' pleaded Rosa. 'Look how clever she's been in finding us. She might be helpful!'

Nan grumbled and lay back, removing her glasses.

'We will discuss this in the morning,' she said, closing her eyes.

It wasn't long before Nan was snoring again but, with Stick at her side, Rosa had no trouble in finding sleep.

3
The Mist

Rosa woke to find the world covered in white. Mist hovered below Wolf Tor like a thick blanket, rolling and billowing along. Occasional tufts lifted up and drifted past at head height. Stick growled at them angrily.

'It's like being above the clouds!' said Rosa.

'It's very unhelpful,' said Nan, rolling

up her damp sleeping bag. Dew had settled on everything overnight and had done nothing for Nan's hair, which was standing on end and even wilder than usual. 'But you get this sort of thing a lot at the coast. It happens when the warm summer air hits the cold sea.'

'How will we find our way?' asked Rosa.

'We'll do our best,' said Nan.

She looked up at the sky and found the sun, rising in the east.

'Aim for the sun, and we should find the coast,' she said.

'But we won't see the sun in the mist,' said Rosa.

Nan smiled and pulled a little metal compass from her pocket.

'Just in case,' she said.

They slipped and stumbled down the tor and on to the plain, where they could see only a few metres ahead with the sun just a dull, distant glow above them. The tall grass was dripping wet, and their trouser legs were instantly soaked.

'Stay close,' said Rosa, patting Stick. The wolf yipped and did exactly as asked.

With Nan taking the lead, they walked for nearly an hour before the mist thinned. But when Rosa was finally able

to see again, it was absolutely worth the wait. The edges of Prickly Plain sloped downwards towards a wide, glistening estuary, dotted with rocky outcrops and thin streams of a river, widening out like the roots of a tree into the deep blue sea.

'And there's the ocean!' said Nan, thrusting her hands on to her hips. She breathed it in, letting her chest fill to bursting with the light, salty air.

'It just goes on forever,' said Rosa.

The coastline was as majestic as Big Sky Mountain itself, curving outwards into the distance and the ocean. Cliffs rose and fell at the land's edge, sometimes crumbling into towering rocky needles that formed broken lines into the sea.

As Rosa cast her eyes along the coast she paused at a red-and-white-striped lighthouse that sat like an exclamation mark at the end of a broken, rocky headland, far out at sea.

'Toe-Dipper Bay,' said Nan. 'And that's Talltop Lighthouse. Legend has it Old Boar Bill used to run it, but it's long abandoned now.'

'Imagine living out there,' said Rosa. 'You really would be all alone.'

'Even more remote than living in a cabin, I should imagine,' said Nan.

Stick sat silently, staring out into the distance. Her ears twitched as a red butterfly flapped silently past. Normally she would have raced after it, but not now, not with that sight in front of her.

'What do you think, Stick?' asked Rosa.

The wolf howled happily. Seeing the sea was enough to cure anyone's worries.

'Now then,' said Nan. 'We best find out who is in trouble!'

They walked the steepening slope down to the estuary. Nan kept her telescope at hand, one eye always on the sea.

'Looks like we've picked the right weather for it,' said Nan, wiping a bead of sweat from her brow.

Rosa had only been to the seaside a few times in her life, but it had been nothing like the seaside on Big Sky Mountain. This sea was rugged and wild, and felt a little bit dangerous. There were no coastguards, and no flags to tell you where was safe to swim.

'Is the tide out?' asked Rosa.

'Looks it,' said Nan, staring up along the beach. 'Though it doesn't go out far here. You won't see much difference, unless you're out on a boat, hoping to navigate the rocks.'

Nan lifted her telescope to her eye and huffed.

'What on earth's all that junk?' she said.

She passed the telescope to Rosa, who gazed at the beach. A zigzag line of brightly-coloured plastic waste stretched for as far as the eye could see.

'It looks like a load of old bottles and rubbish,' she said.

'But what's it doing here?' said Nan.

They followed the edge of the estuary northwards to the sandy beach. What once had been a pristine, beautiful environment was devastated with rubbish.

'It's like a landfill site!' said Nan, stopping to pick up small pieces of plastic. There were lengths of fishing net, tangled around branches of driftwood, crushed milk bottles half buried in the sand, torn biscuit wrappers – you name it, if it was made of plastic, it was there on the beach.

Nan sat down on the sand, utterly distraught.

'Who could have done this?' she said.

Stick came running into sight, a fizzy pop bottle clenched in her teeth. She dropped it at Rosa's feet and ran off to pick up another.

'Let's collect as much as we can,' said
Rosa.

'I agree,' said Nan. 'We can't leave it
like this.'

But before they could begin, they were
startled by a very loud greeting.

'Cooo-eee!' called a voice.
'Helloooooo!'

Rosa squeaked a sharp cry of fear as

a sea monster lurched
out of the water.
It was green and
mossy, with huge
long strands of
brown hair, and it
was waving its arms
frantically.

'What are you!?' she cried.

Nan held out her walking stick and
leapt in front of Rosa to defend her as the
creature walked on to the beach.

'It has brown furry feet . . .' said Nan,
quizzically.

'What?' said Rosa, poking her head
out from behind Nan.

'Hello, hello, hello!' it said cheerfully.

A cute brown paw emerged from

the mass of wet, rubbery green fronds and swept them aside to reveal a chirpy golden face with bright eyes, tiny ears and some deadly sharp teeth.

Grandma Nan laughed out loud.

'It's a sea otter!' she said, lowering her stick.

'What did you think I was?' said the creature, pulling more of the vegetation free to reveal its shape.

'A monster!' said Rosa.

Then the otter rushed straight up to Nan, gripped her hand and shook it violently. Cold, salty seawater rained down on Nan and Rosa.

'Very nice to meet you,' said Nan.

The otter slapped Rosa's shoulder playfully and patted Stick on the head.

The wolf wasn't too sure of the new creature, but she soon warmed to him.

'You too!' he said. 'And aren't you all a sight for sore eyes! My name's Oki. What a joy it is to get visitors.'

'I didn't think anyone lived out here any more,' said Nan.

'There are a few of us now,' said Oki. 'Most are out working in the sea fields. It's not been the easiest of starts, but we're making a good go of it.'

'A go of what?' asked Rosa.

Oki thrust a handful of the colourful vegetation he was carrying under Rosa's nose. It smelled wonderfully green and salty.

'We're seaweed farmers!' he said excitedly, running his paw through the

ribbons of seaweed.
'We grow a few
different sorts,
and they all
seem to thrive
around here.'
'Just like all
this mess on the
beach!' said Nan.

'It comes in on the tide,' said Oki,
angrily. 'No sooner do we clear it all up
than it washes in, all over again.'

'Infuriating,' said Nan.

'Some of it is quite useful,' said Oki.
'We can build things with it, and even
grow things in it. But in truth, we're
swamped in human rubbish.'

'Is that why you fired the flare

yesterday?' said Rosa. 'Asking for help?'

'A flare?' said Oki. 'Not us. We must have missed that, but then we do spend a lot of time underwater.'

'Well, that is very strange,' said Nan. 'Who could it have been?'

'We could have a look from the top of the lighthouse, if you like,' said Oki. 'It's where we sea otters live. You can see most of the mountain from up there. If someone's in trouble, we might spot them.'

Nan thought of her old legs. 'Well, it's quite a long way up!' she said, staring at the top of the lighthouse.

Rosa was excited about seeing inside it. It would be a bit of a climb, she thought, but it would be a real achievement to make it to the top.

'You walk the mountain all day long,' she argued. 'What are you worried about?'

'I suppose you're right,' Nan replied, chuckling at Rosa's determination. 'Come on, then!'

Rosa called Stick to follow, and together with Oki they marched along the beach towards the lighthouse, picking up bits of rubbish as they went.

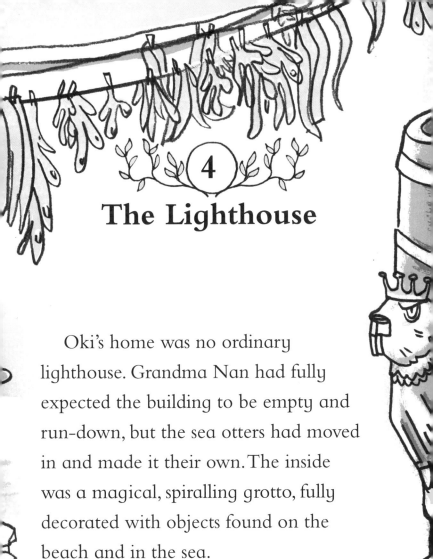

4

The Lighthouse

Oki's home was no ordinary lighthouse. Grandma Nan had fully expected the building to be empty and run-down, but the sea otters had moved in and made it their own. The inside was a magical, spiralling grotto, fully decorated with objects found on the beach and in the sea.

Huge plastic barrels were attached

to drainpipes to catch rainwater, battered old treasure chests had been repurposed for kitchen cupboards and stained-glass windows were formed of little shards of sea-glass. If something was useful, it was in use –

46

and if something was beautiful, it was on display.

'How long have you lived here?' asked Rosa, tugging gently at a curtain made from a tatty piece of old sail.

'About three years,' said Oki, hanging out the seaweed to dry on long lines of rope that stretched from one side of the lighthouse to the other. 'The place was empty and falling apart, so we fixed it up and moved in. You can't keep a sea otter down, that's for sure.'

'I think someone called Old Boar Bill used to live here,' said Nan. 'Legend says he got so lonely –'

'Out here? With the sea?' interrupted Oki, in astonishment. 'Who could ever be lonely with the sea as a friend? It brings you gifts each day, and sings you to sleep at night!'

'Oki sounds like you, Nan,' said Rosa. 'You never get lonely or bored of being on your own.'

'Very true!' said Nan.

Once the sea otter had hung up the last of the seaweed he opened a wooden door, revealing a narrow staircase.

'Ready?' he said. 'We haven't managed to fix the light yet, but the view is as clear as day from the top.'

They walked up the many hundreds of steps that spiralled upwards around the building. Nan found the going tough, but she wasn't one to complain, and Rosa gripped the handrail as tight as she could to feel safe. Stick bounced up behind her, seemingly having no problems at all.

The lighthouse had six floors, each narrower than the last, and the staircase cut through them all on its course to the light room at its top. Eventually, they stepped out into blazing daylight. You could see everything for miles on end. White seabirds with black caps swooped on the wind at their eye level, shouting hello at them as they whizzed past.

'Well, I never!' said Nan, out of puff and propping her hands on her hips.

'Best view on the east coast,' said Oki.
Completely surrounded by glass, Rosa looked out and gulped.
It was a long way down, no matter how wonderful the view.

'Are we safe up here?' she asked, tapping the glass, half expecting the window pane to fall out.

'The lighthouse has been here at least a hundred years,' said Nan, calmly. 'I can't imagine anything happening to it today.'

'You're absolutely right,' said Oki. 'The sea changes by the hour – you could be swimming on its calm, pancake-flat surface one minute, and the next it's like a raging, whipped meringue. But through all that, this lighthouse stays true and tall. It's as hard as iron!'

Nan took out her telescope and scoured the horizon. There were many small islands – none particularly habitable – but one caught her eye.

'What's that really dangerous-looking island?' she asked. 'The one with all the sharp-looking cliffs?'

'That'll be Jagged Rock Island,' said Oki. 'Strange creatures live out there, I can tell you!'

What started with a cluster of tall spiky rocks grew into a bulging outcrop, covered with tufts of grass and boulders.

Nan spotted a few broken planks of wood in one of the rocky coves.

'They could be signs of a wreck,' she said, passing the telescope to Rosa. 'I can't see any life with my old eyes, though. Can you spot anything, Rosa?'

Rosa looked out towards Jagged Rock Island. Waves broke against the beach, sending a spray of white droplets into the air. Suddenly, a large, bright yellow waterproof hat popped up from behind a rock, followed by a bright yellow waterproof jacket.

'I see someone!' she cried. 'In yellow!'

Nan grabbed the telescope and soon caught sight of a person, dragging a wooden crate up out of the sea.

'Well, blow me down,' she said. 'Good spot, Rosa! I reckon they would've sent up the flare!'

'Must have run aground,' said Oki. 'Wouldn't be the first, and won't be the last.'

He tapped the huge bulb in the centre of the room with his short claws.

'I must get this light working,' he added.

'The sea can be so dangerous without a lighthouse to guide the boats safely into shore,' said Nan. She thought quietly for a moment. 'I don't like their chances out there. Whoever it is, we'll have to go and rescue them.'

'Out there?' said Rosa. 'How would we get there?'

'A boat?' asked Nan.

Oki scratched his bristly cheek and let out a sigh.

'We don't have anything like that round here,' he said. 'We otters just don't need boats. But even if we did have one, that's a tough island to reach.'

'We'll have to improvise, then,' said Nan.

Rosa remembered all the plastic bottles and barrels littering the beach, and she had a terrific idea.

'We could build a raft out of all the junk on the beach!' she said. 'We could use some of those nets to hold it all together – we all know that plastic floats and, if nothing else, it'll help clear the rubbish up a little.'

'What a wonderful idea,' said Nan, with a wink.

'I like it!' said Oki. 'I definitely have a few old oars lying around. There are some nasty currents to navigate too, but we can guide you through the worst of them!'

Rosa pushed her face against the glass and looked down upon the forest of seaweed in the water a short distance from shore. It swayed like hair in a bath, caught up in the swirling current, and just watching it move made her stomach wobble. She could see how difficult sailing across to the island would be.

'What say you, Rosa?' asked Nan.

Rosa took a deep breath. 'I don't think we have a choice, do we?' she replied. 'We have to!'

Oki's eyes opened wide, and he gestured excitedly to the doorway.

'Don't you worry,' he said. 'I have just the things to keep you safe!'

5

The Raft

Oki and his family collected up some
of the larger plastic barrels on the beach,
as well as a fine collection of smooth
driftwood and lengths of plastic rope. He
then hurried back inside and returned
with three bright orange life jackets, one
much smaller than the others.

'They were hanging on the wall of
the lighthouse,' he said, patting one of the

jackets. 'They should fit you perfectly!'

Nan slipped one on over her head, and Rosa copied her. She immediately felt more assured.

'What do you think?' asked Nan.

'Much better,' said Rosa, as Nan tightened the cords around her front. 'But what's this?'

She held up a small whistle tied to its front.

'You blow it if you're in trouble,' said Nan.

'I see,' said Rosa, giving it a go.

Stick jumped to attention at the screeching whistle, and Rosa apologised with a forced smile.

'And this tiny one,' said Oki, holding the mini life jacket aloft, 'is for the wolf!'

Rosa clapped excitedly.

'Stick gets her own life jacket?!' she cried.

'Why not?' said Nan.

Stick stood up proudly so that Oki could fasten the little jacket around her. Then she howled in delight and ran round in a circle.

They started work on the raft immediately, tying the barrels together

first, and then strapping lengths of
wood together to make a deck.

It quickly took shape, and Stick
leapt up on top.

'Captain Stick!' said Rosa,
standing to attention with a
salute.

Stick wagged her tail
happily.

'It's looking solid,' said
Nan, kicking the barrels
firmly. 'Should see us to the
island and cope with another
passenger, as well!'

'There's only one way to
find out!' said Oki.

Oki tied a rope to the front
of the raft and, with Rosa's help,

dragged it down the beach towards the frothing surf. A crab looked at them in confusion, muttered a few grumpy words and scuttled out of their way to safety.

'On you get!' said Oki, holding the raft firmly while Rosa clambered on. Nan climbed up, perhaps not finding it as easy as she might have done in her youth, and found her sea legs.

'All good!' she said, wobbling a little. 'It's not Florence, but it'll do.'

'We need a name for it,' said Rosa. 'Something epic and adventurous! Something sea-monstery . . .'

Nan thought that was a terrific idea. She hummed and hawed, deep in thought.

'The Leviathan . . . the Nautilus . . . the –'

'How about the Sea Squirt?' said Oki, with a cheeky grin.

Rosa spat out a laugh. It was exactly the opposite to what she was imagining, but it felt perfect. Nan's smile widened across her face as the name sank in.

'I think that suits us perfectly,' she said, laughing.

'All aboard the Sea Squirt for her maiden voyage!' said Rosa.

Oki jerked the rope to get the raft moving. It scraped and bobbed as it slid to the sea and, as the waves hit its side, a spray of water covered Rosa. It was cold but thrilling, and Rosa loved it.

The waves fought back against Oki's strength, making it difficult to get the raft fully out into the open sea. But with Nan and Rosa providing some extra push from the oars, they eventually slipped past the breakers.

Oki swam alongside, playfully dipping under the raft and surprising Rosa as he popped up further out or closer in. Sea otters clearly liked to have fun, thought Rosa.

Jagged Rock Island was still a distant lump on the horizon, and it approached slowly as the tide and current pushed and pulled the raft in every way.

'Are we actually moving anywhere?' asked Rosa, pulling the oar through the water.

'I know it feels like it's making no difference,' said Nan, 'but it's just the sea playing tricks on us.'

Three other otters joined Oki, chattering to each other above the sound of the swooshing sea. Something seemed to be going on, and Rosa started to worry.

'All right! Hold tight!' cried Oki, as he and the other otters gripped on to the side of the raft for safety. 'Marge is on the move!'

'Who's Marge?' said Rosa.

A gigantic oblong-shaped shadow grew darker in the sea alongside them.

'Here she comes!' said Oki.

The raft lurched upwards in the swelling sea, and Rosa dropped to the deck, gripping Stick tight.

'A whale!' said Nan, excitedly, clutching her oar for balance.

A huge blue whale breached the water and fired a squirt of white froth high into the air from her blowhole.

'Morning, Marge!' said Oki, bobbing up and down rapidly on the surface.

The whale groaned 'HELLO!' and disappeared again under the water, leaving a thick trail of foul-smelling gunk in her wake.

'URGH!' spat Rosa. 'What's that?'

'I think she just did an unbelievably, extraordinarily large whale-sized poo,' said Nan.

Oki covered his nose with his paw and scrambled up on to the Sea Squirt. The other otters did the same, for fear of getting covered in the strange goop floating through the sea.

'Couldn't she have used a toilet?' asked Rosa, covering her nose.

As the choppy waters calmed, they

used the oars again and drifted on.

Oki checked the water quality –
staring at it, then sniffing it.

'I wouldn't want to swim in it, but
Marge feeds whole armies of creatures
with that . . .'

He struggled to find the right word.

'Poo!' said Rosa.

'Exactly,' he replied. 'It sinks down
through the water, providing food for
animals at every level. Without
her, many creatures would go
hungry.'

'They eat it?' asked Rosa, appalled.

'I guess they don't know much better,'
said Oki, laughing. 'Or maybe they think
it tastes delicious? I don't know.'

'Urgh!' said Rosa.

Even Stick turned up her nose at that suggestion, and she was well known for rolling in all manner of horrible things.

'Isn't the sea amazing?' said Nan. 'It's no different to the land, really. There are barren deserts, where nothing can live, and there are forests and cities down there, too. But we're all dependent on each other, ultimately.'

Oki ran his paw through the water and, deciding it was now safe, he dived in, followed by the other sea otters. His head popped out of the water.

'You should be all right from here,' he said. 'We have work to do, but we'll keep an eye out for storms and bad weather and come help if you need it!'

Nan saluted, in true seafaring style.

'Thanks, Oki! It's not far now,' she said, enjoying the salty breeze against her face. 'Come on, Rosa, just a little further!'

They pulled on their oars with greater strength, driving the Sea Squirt ever closer to their destination. But with that came a new type of danger – the rocks!

'Hold on tight, Stick!' said Rosa, seeing the tips of black, barnacled rocks rise above the waves then disappear. 'Danger ahead!'

Nan held her oar firm in the water to slow the raft.

'We need to land in one piece or there'll be no getting home,' she said. 'So keep your eyes peeled, my girl, and let's go carefully.'

'Aye aye, Captain!' said Rosa, and she settled in for the ride.

6

Jagged Rock Island

There was much more to Jagged Rock Island than either Nan or Rosa could have seen from the lighthouse. It loomed over them like a dark, bulging loaf of bread, while at its edges treacherous rocks pierced up through the sea like needles.

'Hard to port side!' said Nan, spying a safe passage to shore.

'To the what?' said Rosa, confused.

'To the left!' said Nan. 'If you're facing the front of the ship, port is always the left side, starboard the right. Got it?'

'OK!' said Rosa. 'Hard to port, Captain!'

Rosa steered the raft as best she could, but the currents and rocks made it tricky – not to mention confusing, with all the sailing words Nan was determined to use. If they ever got too close to a rock, Stick would dash from side to side of the raft, pushing them away with her little paws

They made a good team, and they slowly drifted to safety.

As they drew nearer to shore, the remains of the wrecked boat were clear to see, with planks and shards of wood littering the water.

'One last push,' said Nan, reaching out to a boulder.

She took hold, and then stepped across with the rope in her hand. With a sharp tug, the Sea Squirt ran aground on the steep, gravelly beach. Rosa hooked Stick under her arm and jumped down to help Nan drag the raft higher up above the waterline.

'We made it!' said Rosa.

'Quite the adventure,' said Nan. 'And now to find our castaway! Let's explore!'

Stick sniffed the ground ferociously, searching for a scent, as Rosa inhaled the joy of the island. It felt even more remote than Nan's cabin, but she also knew that it would be teeming with new creatures she'd never seen before.

Rosa heard a strange little clacking
noise from behind a rock, and went
to investigate. The narrow shore, lined
with water-sculpted boulders, was full of
rockpools and nooks and secret caves. It
was a treasure-seeker's dream, rich with
shells and seaweed of all kinds.

'Hello?' said Rosa, happily. 'Is anyone
there?'

She skipped through a huge rock that had been cleft in two, and chanced upon the most peculiar sight. A line of hermit crabs, of various sizes and in various types of shell, were in deep discussion.

'You can have my one,' said a crab. 'It's your size.'

'No, no, you're much bigger,' said another.

'You lot don't know what you're talking about, I'm clearly the biggest,' argued a third, muscling into the line.

Then a fourth crab, with shiny black eyes, hesitantly scampered into view. This crab wore the strangest shell of all – in fact, Rosa wasn't certain it even was a shell. It looked to her like a squat plastic milk bottle.

'Oh no, it's Larry,' said one of the crabs, shifting away from this newcomer. The others all looked furtively at the crab with the strange shell.

'I don't want anything to do with him,' said one of them, rudely. She pointed at his shell. 'You wouldn't catch me dead me in a horrorshow shell like that!'

Rosa felt desperately sad for the crab

in the weird attire; so sad that she decided there and then to stage an intervention.

'Why do you all have to be so mean?' she asked, surprising the crabs with her presence.

They retreated into their shells and fell deathly silent.

'I can see you all, you know,' she said, walking closer and tapping on each shell with her index finger. 'Why were you all being so mean?'

The crabs stayed resolutely locked in their shells. Rosa crossed her arms defiantly.

'If you think I'm going away, you're very mistaken,' she said.

The little crab with the strange shell peered out from his very obvious hiding place.

'H-Hello?' he said, worriedly.

'It's Larry, isn't it?' asked Rosa, bending down. 'Is everything all right?'

The crab popped his head and claws out of his shell and tentatively clacked his way towards her. Rosa was now certain that his shell really was a faded old plastic milk bottle, and it set him quite apart from the other crabs.

'Not really,' said Larry, sadly. 'They don't like my shell.'

'Why does that matter?' asked Rosa.

'We all swap shells as we grow bigger,'

he said. 'We recycle them – the bigger crabs pass theirs down to the smaller crabs.'

'And they don't want yours?' said Rosa.

Larry's pincer-like claws tapped together sadly.

'They say it's not a real shell, so they won't swap with me,' he said. 'But I'm getting too big for it now and I need a new one. I don't know what to do!'

Rosa knew full well that it wasn't a real shell, but she also knew it was mean of the other crabs to push Larry away.

'Why don't I help you find a new one?' she said.

Larry's little black eyes shot up on their stalks.

'Do you mean it?' he asked.

'There must be hundreds around here,' she said. 'Come with me!'

Larry proudly set off behind Rosa while the other crabs hid in their shells. They scoured the beach, Rosa picking up one shell after another and suggesting them to Larry. Nothing was quite big enough. After a few minutes, Rosa found what she thought was the perfect fit. It was striped in shimmering colours, and would certainly make Larry stand out amongst the others.

'How about this?!' she said, placing it on the ground.

Larry nestled up alongside the shell and checked its measurements like you might hold a pair of trousers against you for size. He'd certainly not made a home in such a fancy shell before. He flipped it over and tapped it to make sure it was strong enough. It was.

'I think it's beautiful!' he said. 'Shall I try it on?'

'Of course!' said Rosa.

She turned away to save any blushes, and Larry discarded the milk bottle and skipped into the new shell. It really was special. He stood up proudly.

'You can look now,' he said.

Rosa turned around and cheered. Larry now looked like the most amazing crab of all. His new outfit would have been perfect for a night out at a disco.

'I think you should go and show the others,' she said.

Larry hurried off towards the group
of crabs, who were finally starting to
come out of their shells. Then he scuttled
straight past them.

'Is that Larry?' said one, ogling Larry's
shell.

'I want it!' said another, jealously.
'Larry, swap with me!'

A third, smaller crab, barged into Larry.

'Give it to me,' he said. 'Larry, give it to me!'

But Larry just marched on towards the sea, oblivious to their calls. His shell shone more brightly and more glamorously than all the others, and it was the most wonderful new home.

7
The Castaway

When Rosa found Nan and Stick, they were hiking up a steep, narrow path, made over many years by the tread of some unknown creatures. In any other place on the mainland, it would have been a goat or sheep path, but there didn't seem to be any mammals on this island.

'Find anything?' asked Nan,

clambering upwards. Her feet slipped on the gravelly slope, which wasn't fit for human weight.

'Some hermit crabs,' said Rosa, trying to catch up.

'Friendly?' asked Nan.

'One was,' said Rosa.

Then Stick shot off, her tail pointing to the skies.

'What is it, girl?' said Rosa, hurrying up the path.

The route gradually levelled out on to the top of the island – a scrubby, grassy knoll, dotted with low gorse bushes and hardy little wildflowers. There was no shelter, apart from a few dips and hollows. Stick bounded across the grass and disappeared over the other side.

Rosa cried out with worry, but she needn't have bothered.

The yellow hat appeared above the grassy edge, followed by the rest of the creature in the yellow rain mac. Stick reappeared and started running circles around the creature's two furry legs.

'Well, I never,' said Nan. 'It's you!'

'Mr Hibberdee!' said Rosa, overjoyed.

Mr Hibberdee was Nan and Rosa's old friend – a travelling sales bear who did a particularly fine line in biscuits and crackers, and any other treats one might enjoy. He was not usually found at sea!

'I knew you'd save me!' called Mr Hibberdee, waving furiously.

He skipped over to Nan, lifted her up and spun her around in joy.

'What on earth are you doing out here?!' she asked, giddily.

'It was a mistake!' he said, placing her

down. 'A huge mistake . . . Well, I say that. When you see what delights I have you'll realise the risk was worth it!'

'Risk?' said Nan. 'What have you been up to?'

'Creating a new trade route,' said Mr Hibberdee, with great seriousness. 'I received notice of a new biscuit – more crunchy, more fruity and simply better than any other – but in order to get them I had to travel down the coast. So I thought I'd sail!'

'Have you ever been in a boat?' asked Rosa.

'Not exactly, though I bought the right clothes for it,' he replied, as if owning a waterproof jacket was all it took to be a sailor.

'You were very irresponsible,' said Nan, shaking her head.

'It wasn't my fault this stupid island popped up out of nowhere!' he said.

However silly Mr Hibberdee was to set out on a voyage without any experience, Rosa was still very happy to see him. She ran up to him and squeezed him tight.

'I'm very pleased you're still in one piece,' she said, happily.

Mr Hibberdee grew incredibly excited.

'Come! Come!' he said, bouncing up and down on the spot. 'You must try one!'

'Try what?' said Nan.

'The biscuits!' said Mr Hibberdee.

They all followed the bear across the little island and down the other side into a rugged cove. He'd made a perfect little home for himself, using half of his broken boat tipped up on end as a shelter. There were the remnants of a fire, still smouldering, surrounded by wooden crates.

Rosa was quick to spot that one of the crates had been prised open. She peered inside and saw boxes and boxes of neatly packaged biscuits. The crate was only half full.

'How many have you eaten already?' she asked. There were crumbs clinging to the bear's fur as clear as day.

'Very, very few,' said Mr Hibberdee, lying. 'But I was hungry and feared I'd be trapped here forever!'

'Surely you'd want them to last as long as possible if that was the case?' said Nan.

Mr Hibberdee had never been one for making things last, especially biscuits. He sniffed and shrugged.

'Tea?' he said.

He dragged a large red case into view and opened the lock. It was full of useful implements, as well as a box of tea.

'What's all that in there?' asked Nan.

'My emergency survival box,' he said. 'It came with the boat. It was a good thing I had it, too!'

He showed Grandma Nan the empty case of a flare.

'If I hadn't shot this flare into the sky I'd be a goner!'

Then Mr Hibberdee relit the fire with matches from his box, and spooned tea leaves into a tiny traveller's teapot.

'Do you have water?' asked Nan.

'We're surrounded by it,' said Mr Hibberdee.

Rosa was confused.

'You can't drink seawater,' she said.

'Ridiculous,' he replied. 'Course you can.'

Grandma Nan shook her head and delved into her backpack.

'You'll never make a good sea bear,' she said, removing her flask of drinking water. 'Seawater is full of salt, and terribly bad for you. You don't drink it, not even as a last resort!'

'What? That's madness!' said Mr Hibberdee.

'Grandma Nan knows her stuff,' said Rosa. 'Since when have you known her to be wrong about things like this?'

Mr Hibberdee huffed and stomped down to the water's edge. He scooped up a handful of seawater and took a sip.

'BLEURGH!' he cried, spitting out the water.

'Told you,' said Nan.

Mr Hibberdee looked crestfallen. He hated looking stupid, and Rosa was quick to notice.

'You weren't to know,' she said. 'You're not a sea bear, after all.'

Mr Hibberdee's mood picked up.

'I'm not, but I'd like to be!' he said.

'So would I,' said Rosa.

Nan checked the fire and poured her water into the kettle. She was careful not to use too much.

'We have so little water, we can't stay long on the island,' she said, poking the bristling flame with a piece of wood. 'But we'll have enough to see out the night. I don't fancy making the crossing in the darkness without that lighthouse to guide us.'

Rosa was quite excited by the thought of spending a night by the sea. At least they had plenty of food.

'We won't go hungry with all the biscuits,' she said.

'Speaking of which . . .' said the bear.

He passed around one of the packets and, as the tea brewed, they chewed away, relishing the rare and wonderful delights of Mr Hibberdee's new stock.

8

Late Night Guests

That night, as Rosa was nestling down to sleep, the sky was filled with a peculiar whooshing noise that swirled above them. It was as though the sound of the sea had risen upwards. She sat bolt upright, and noticed that Nan and Mr Hibberdee were doing the same.

'Hold on to your hats!' said Nan.

'What is it?' asked Rosa.

'Incoming!' growled Mr Hibberdee.

Stick ducked into Rosa's sleeping bag for cover.

Looking like a barrage of black-and-white jacket potatoes with wings, a flock of puffins tumbled out of the sky and landed right on top of the campsite.

'Oh my days! We have trespassers!' chirped a particularly serious bird with a very un-serious, brightly coloured beak.

She poked Grandma Nan's feet inside the sleeping bag, then swivelled sharply to poke Rosa's.

'Hello?' said Rosa, a little uneasily.

'This is the holiday home of the Buffin family!' said the puffin, leaning forward so that her beak pressed up against Rosa's nose. 'Humans and bears are definitely not allowed!'

'OK . . .' said Rosa, as fearful as anyone can be of a bird with such a colourful, cheerful face. 'And you're a Buffin?'

'Mrs Buffin, if you please!' said the bird.

Stick peered out from the sleeping bag, sniffing the air cautiously.

'And wolves are not allowed either!' said the puffin.

'We're not planning on staying long,' said Nan, calming the bird. 'You don't need to worry.'

Mrs Buffin waddled away to talk to her friends and family. They chattered amongst themselves.

'Well, all right, then,' she said, turning back. 'But to stay here you must pay us with some of your food. You do have some, don't you?'

Mr Hibberdee laughed.

'A kindred spirit!' he said. He rooted around for some of his biscuits and handed them out.

Mrs Buffin took six in her beak – a feat of prowess that impressed even Mr Hibberdee, who could only fit three biscuits in his mouth at any one time.

'How on earth can you do that?' he said, in awe.

'Very special tongues,' mumbled the puffin. She returned to her group and handed them out.

'Delicious, delicious,' she said, struggling to speak.

Mr Hibberdee nudged Grandma Nan.

'I told you they were the best biscuits,'

he whispered. He rubbed his paws. 'Looks like I've got some new customers!'

'I'm not sure they're that keen on paying for things,' said Nan.

'Any more?' said Mrs Buffin, returning in a sprightly manner.

Nan arched an eyebrow, knowingly. The bear shrugged.

'Why not?' he said, handing over a few more biscuits. He cast a glance towards Nan. He was feeling very confident about this customer-in-the-making.

'Thank you, thank you,' said the puffin.

Mr Hibberdee made a big display of closing the packet of biscuits and tucking them away. Then, as the puffins waddled

off to find a place to sleep, Mr Hibberdee
lay back down and Grandma Nan did
the same.

Rosa had a smile on her face, but was
struggling to stay awake and nestled back
down to rest. The sound of the sea was
better than anything for dreaming along
to, and within minutes she was soundly
asleep.

9

Puffed and Stuffed

The misty morning came with the swift realisation that puffins and biscuits are a dangerous mix. Mr Hibberdee's face was a picture.

'They've eaten them all!' he said furiously. He plodded back and forth, tossing empty and torn biscuit packets in the air. Stick collected them up, catching them mid-flight like they were snowflakes on his tongue.

Nan covered her mouth with her hand to stop herself laughing. All the full crates had been pecked open, meaning Mr Hibberdee's sea-faring efforts had been for nothing. And as for Mrs Buffin and the puffins, they were flat out on their backs, fast asleep, their bellies swollen from all the biscuits. They looked very pleased with themselves.

'Aren't there any left?' asked Rosa.

'Not even a crumb,' said Mr Hibberdee.

He collapsed on to his bottom and looked out forlornly over the ocean.

'I'll have to buy another boat,' he said. 'Then I'll have to go back and buy some more!'

Rosa patted him on the back as tears

welled in his sad eyes.

'I'm not sure it's worth it,' she said, calmly. 'There must be other ways. Other exciting new treats?'

'There are none,' said the bear.

Grandma Nan picked up her things and walked up to the top of the island. Wind whipped over her head, lifting the sea into little white peaks and driving a thin mist across the island. It wasn't ideal conditions for sailing a raft, but they were low on drinking water and, worst of all, a bank of darker clouds hung on the horizon.

She walked back to Rosa, passing the puffins on the way. In between snores, Mrs Buffin burped louder than you'd imagine a little seabird could ever burp.

'We should get ready to sail,' said Nan. 'I think we may only have a short time before a storm rolls in. The wind will help us reach the bay.'

'The sooner the better!' said Mr Hibberdee, still in a grump. He cast an angry glance at the puffed-up puffins – who barely stirred – and collected his

things. Without biscuits to carry, all he had was his emergency pack and his raincoat and hat.

They crossed the island back to the raft and checked it was still in good shape.

'Tighten all the ropes,' said Nan, tapping each plank to test it for movement. 'We'll need the raft to be proper shipshape!'

Mr Hibberdee fiddled with knots while Rosa set to work tugging ropes and kicking the floats underneath to check they hadn't filled with water. Even Stick got involved, biting into ropes and pulling them. Nothing moved. The Sea Squirt was shipshape all right.

'I reckon it should hold us all,' said Nan, happily.

'Well, I don't care,' said Mr Hibberdee, still feeling aggrieved. 'I just want to get off this silly island.'

Rosa lifted Stick on to the raft, then hung back as Nan and Mr Hibberdee climbed on. She thought it would be easy to push the raft down the slope alone, but all she managed was a little skid before it ground to a halt.

'You're all too heavy,' said Rosa.

Mr Hibberdee dropped down to push, but he too struggled to get much movement out of the raft.

'Can I help?' said a kind, quiet voice to Rosa's side.

Rosa looked down and found Larry the hermit crab, ready to provide some muscle.

'Hello again,' she said.

'This shell is the best home I've ever had,' he said. 'Everyone else is jealous. They keep following me around and asking me to swap.'

'I bet,' said Rosa. 'You do look very smart.'

Larry clacked his claw.

'Right, then. Where do I push?' he asked.

'Anywhere!' said Rosa.

On the count of three they heaved and ho-ed, but though the raft had nearly reached the sea by now it was very slow going, and it still needed a little more wallop.

'I should help,' said Nan.

Stick wagged her tail and whined, to let them know that she wanted to help too.

'No, no,' said Rosa. 'I don't want either of you getting hurt. The sea is really choppy now.'

Then the little hermit crab took action.

'Wait here!' said Larry.

And within a few minutes he'd
returned with all the other hermit crabs
on the island. There were twenty at least,
and they all took hold of the raft, ready
to push.

'I persuaded them by saying next time you visited you'd find them all shells like mine,' he said.

'That sounds fair!' said Mr Hibberdee.

Rosa agreed.

Together they pushed, and eventually the raft bobbed out on to the water. Mr Hibberdee and Rosa leapt on. They waved goodbye to the island and their new friends, strapped on their life jackets and paddled as fast as they could. The sea looked to be getting rougher by the second, and the dark clouds were chasing them out into open water.

Nan forced her oar through the water. The wind was with them, but they still didn't feel like they were getting anywhere fast.

'I'd hoped the sea would be kinder,' she said. 'But don't worry, let's keep pushing on.'

The bear used his giant paws as oars, and even Stick tried to help, though her little paws couldn't reach the water. The waves lifted them higher and higher, and the sky darkened.

'Here we go,' said Nan. 'Hold on tight!'

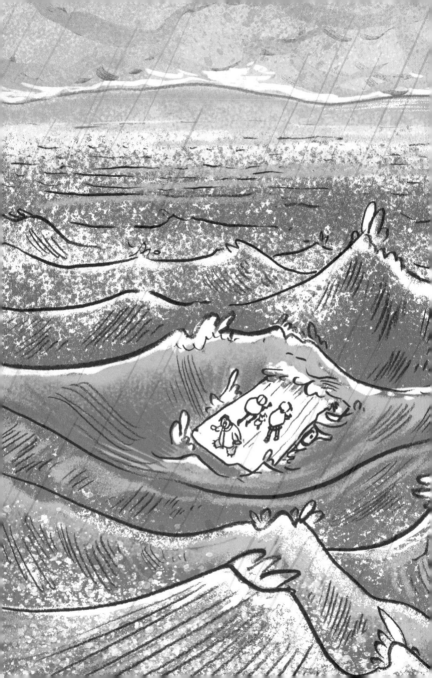

All at Sea

The rain flew down, blasting craters into the rising waves. Rosa was now feeling seasick and scared, and it was getting harder and harder to paddle. The coast was starting to look a long way away. She knelt down to keep her balance.

'Nan, are we going to be all right?' she asked, hugging Stick to her. Mr Hibberdee also huddled closer for safety, tucking the edge of his raincoat over Stick to keep her dry.

Grandma Nan swayed to balance herself as the raft climbed a wave and splashed down the other side.

'I think so,' she said. But from the tone of her voice, Rosa knew she was also worried.

Nan finally pulled the oar from the water and sat down alongside the others. Their fate was now in the hands of the sea.

'We should blow the whistles,' said Rosa.

The raft kept dipping below the tall waves, and they kept losing sight of land. Despite their raincoats they were soaked through and water kept crashing down on to the deck, making it slippery and dangerous.

'I think so, too,' said Nan, placing her arm around Rosa for comfort. 'Follow my timing!'

They both took a deep breath and blew as hard as they could.

PEEP! PEEP! PEEP!

PAAAAARP PAAAAARP PAAAAARP!

PEEP! PEEP! PEEP!

'And again,' said Nan, inhaling once more.

Rosa joined in again and again until Stick could bear no more whistling. Her paws were stuck fully into her ears, and she let out a little howl of unhappiness. Wave after wave crashed over the raft and, each time, everyone clung on to each other for safety.

The blackened clouds were now fully overhead, casting the sea into a twilight darkness, speckled with frothing peaks of foam. Rosa hoped above all that Oki had heard them, but nowhere could she see his cheerful head, bobbing up and down on the water.

'Are they ever coming?' she asked.

'I don't know,' said Nan. 'But the storm will pass. I know it. Just a little longer!'

The waves grew ever taller, and Rosa

squeezed her eyes shut. It was almost too much to bear. But then something strange and wonderful happened. The waves appeared to shrink, as the raft lifted slowly up into the air.

'What's going on?' said Mr Hibberdee, panicking.

Nan looked out over the side of the raft, and saw that they were hovering a short distance above the water.

'Blow my trumpet!' she said. 'It looks like we're being rescued after all!'

Everyone peered over the side of the raft, which was sitting on top of a very large sea mammal – the one, the only, the absolutely magnificent Marge.

'A whale?!' cried Mr Hibberdee.

'Marge!' said Rosa, joyfully.

'Morning,' groaned Marge, her head
breaking the surface of the water. 'I heard
you were in trouble. Those whistles gave
me an earache! Good job they did, I
suppose . . .'

The whale was powering through the
choppy waters, not at all bothered by the
storm, carrying the raft towards the coast.
Oki and his family had also heard the
calls for help, and swam out to greet them

as the raft entered the shallows, allowing Marge to head back out to safer, deeper water.

'S. O. S.,' said Oki, taking hold of the raft. 'Quick thinking!'

'What's S. O. S.?' asked Rosa.

'We whistled it,' said Nan. 'It's Morse Code for Save Our Souls. It's what all boats send out when in distress. It's very useful to know!'

'I'll say,' said Mr Hibberdee. 'Wish I'd known it a few days ago.'

The storm eventually moved on to different shores, and Oki and the sea otters pulled the raft up on to the beach. The sand was awash with a new storm haul of seaweed, shells and tatty bits of netting. There were also two new creatures on shore, who looked distinctly out of place.

'Albert?' said Rosa, climbing down. 'What are you doing all the way out here?'

Albert the Moose stood sadly, his head hung low.

'Searching,' he said, gloomily. 'Forever searching. I lost Stick as soon as you hoomans went on a wander.'

Little Pig leapt off Albert's antlers and dive-bombed Nan and Rosa.

'WHERE HAVE YOU BEEN?!'
he screamed in anger. 'We've been
searching EVERYWHERE for Stick!
EVERYWHERE!'

'Ah . . .' said Nan.

The little wolf crept out sheepishly
from behind Rosa and showed her face.

'YOU HAVE HER?!' screamed Little
Pig.

Stick sat silently, her ears flat back on
her head.

'We're sorry,' said Rosa. 'You must
have travelled miles . . .'

Albert bent his knees and nestled down
on to the ground.

'Albert tired now,' he said.

'I'm not,' screamed Little Pig. 'I'm
FURIOUS!'

Mr Hibberdee stepped off the raft, attempting to calm the owl down.

'I would offer you a fantastic biscuit –' he said.

Little Pig dropped on to the bear's waterproof hat and perched hungrily.

'Yes?' said the pygmy owl, hopefully. He was starving, and it had been a long journey.

'– but a load of puffins ate them all,' Mr Hibberdee finished.

Little Pig rocketed up into the sky in a thunderous rage.

Oki helped Nan down on to the beach. He realised something should be done to cheer everyone up.

'We have a magnificent range of seaweed snacks at the lighthouse,' he said. 'I'm happy to open up our store cupboards!'

Mr Hibberdee's jaw fell open.

'Seaweed snacks?' he said.

'Crunchy ones, squidgy ones, fried ones . . .' said Oki. 'You name it, we've got it.'

'Why didn't you say?' said the bear, rubbing his paws.

Stick bounced over to Albert and howled a sad 'Sorry' into his face. Albert yawned, but he understood its meaning.

'Apples,' he said, closing his eyes. 'Must find apples.'

11

Seaweed Saves the Day

Everyone sat down to eat in the
lighthouse. The table was awash with
seaweed of all shapes and sizes, and
cakes and snacks of equally interesting
proportions: some were round like fruit,
some were square like blocks of cheese,
some were flat like sheets of paper. Mr
Hibberdee had never seen anything quite
so marvellous.

'This surely makes up for all the lost treats,' said Nan, biting into a crispy sheet of dark green seaweed.

Mr Hibberdee was over the moon.

'I can sell these!' he said, picking up each seaweed-based product. 'People will love them!'

'And no more sailing,' said Nan.

'Not until the lighthouse is working again,' he said. 'I promise.'

'Good,' said Nan. 'You were very lucky Rosa spotted the flare.'

'I know, I know!' said Mr Hibberdee, chewing his second piece of seaweed cake. 'Thank you, Rosa.'

Rosa knew how important it was that everyone looked after each other on the mountain.

'We should try and fix the light while we're here,' she said. 'Wouldn't it help everyone?'

'A very good idea!' said Nan. 'Do you know what's wrong with it, Oki?'

The sea otter shrugged. 'The wiring's shot through,' he said. 'But I'm useless at electrics, especially with these paws!'

'We should have a look,' said Nan. 'Rosa's been learning a little bit of wiring.'

When they'd finished eating they marched to the top of the lighthouse, and Oki opened a rusty panel next to the giant bulb. A few grumpy moths flittered out. Something little – and likely furry – had made a wonderful multi-coloured meal of the many wires running from the generator to the gigantic lightbulb.

'Ouch!' said Rosa.

'Yes,' said Nan. 'That will be the problem all right! Those wires'll need replacing. But with what?'

They searched the lighthouse from top to bottom, but found nothing of any use hidden in the rooms. Nan resorted to searching through her backpack, but with little luck. Mr Hibberdee tipped the contents of his emergency bag on to a table, and found that he was prepared for pretty much any eventuality. Nan pushed aside the socks, matches, mint sweets and sunglasses, and picked up a large torch.

'I think this could be just what we're looking for!' she said.

She unscrewed the battery lid and

broke apart the torch's body. With some
help from Little Pig's very sharp beak,
they cut out the wires and set to work
replacing any that needed changing on
the lighthouse generator.

Nan struggled to get her fingers into the little gaps, so she showed Rosa what was required instead. With a bit of guidance from Nan, Rosa twisted old wires into new wires, wrapped them in tape and, before long, all the broken connections were fixed.

'I think that's ready now,' said Rosa, proudly.

Oki looked overjoyed, and ran away to find the 'ON' switch. From the depths of the lighthouse came a deep growling noise as the generator roared into life.

'Watch out!' said Nan.

Suddenly the light burst into life, illuminating the glass room. It slowly turned, and the huge beam of light cut across the top of Rosa's head.

'Amazing!' said Rosa. 'Do you think we'll see it from the cabin?'

'On clear nights, I should think so,' said Nan.

'It'll make the coast feel so much closer!' said Rosa. 'I love it out here.'

'So do I,' said Nan.

12

A Dip in the Bay

Rosa woke up early the next day –
though not as early as Albert, who had
already gone off in search of apples with
Little Pig. Nan was still snoring, and was
battling even Mr Hibberdee for the prize
of loudest sleeper. Light on her feet, Rosa
carried Stick outside to avoid waking the
others. The sun was low in the sky and
cast a dazzling light on to the calm sea.

It was a beautiful morning for rubbish collecting.

Oki led the way along the beach, carrying a rubbish sack over his shoulder and removing anything he spotted. Rosa couldn't believe how much junk washed up each day.

'Is there nothing we can do to stop it?' she asked, placing a piece of plastic pipe in a bag made of old fishing nets.

'You can't stop the tides and currents of the sea,' said Oki. 'Only people can make a difference by not throwing plastic away so carelessly.'

Rosa understood Oki's words, and was determined to do even better from now on. And that meant finding every last little piece that was scattered across

the beach. As she collected bottle tops
and slivers of packaging Rosa heard the
lighthouse door clank open.

Oki laughed aloud.

'There goes your grandma!' he said.

Grandma Nan hurtled down the
beach wearing just her
dark brown swimsuit,
a yellowing white
swimming cap and her
big glasses.

'Coming for a dip,
Rosa?!' cried Nan,
with a wonderful
giggle.

'Now there's an
offer you can't refuse!'
said Oki.

'But won't it be really cold?' said Rosa.

'Not when you have fur,' said Oki, patting his chest.

Rosa suddenly wished she had fur, even if it made her look funny. Nan leapt headfirst into the water, making it look as easy and carefree as stepping into a warm bath.

'I don't know,' Rosa said.

'You'll regret it if you don't,' said Oki and, with that, he dropped his bag of rubbish and raced off to join Nan. Nothing could stop Oki from swimming.

Rosa sighed, but she knew Oki was right. It wasn't every day you got to swim in the sea.

'All right,' she said bravely, pulling her swimsuit from her backpack. 'Wait for me!'

She got changed in a hurry and skipped down the beach. Stick raced her all the way, and hurtled into the white foam of the surf with all the joy of youth. But Stick clearly had never been in the sea before. No sooner had the chilly water penetrated her fur than she leapt back on to dry land with a shiver and a yelp.

Rosa giggled, patting her as she reached the water's edge.

'I know,' she said wisely.

Rosa held out her big toe and dipped it in the water as the lightly breaking waves frothed at her feet.

A chill roared through her foot, but she forced herself to take one tentative step after another.

'Come on!' said Nan. 'It's fine once you're in!'

Nan ducked under the water and reappeared with Oki and his family alongside. The otters knew exactly how to enjoy themselves, darting left and right through the waves like furry torpedoes.

Rosa took a deep breath and clenched her fists.

'There's no whale poo in there, is there?' she said.

'I should imagine it's all been eaten by now!' said Nan, laughing.

Rosa finally threw herself in. The cold was so intense her breath was stolen from

her, but very quickly she felt a warm buzz
rise up from her legs and fill her body.
Oki flipped over playfully and cheered
aloud as Rosa started to swim. The salty

water splashed at her face, but she didn't
care. It was joyful.

'You did it, my girl!' said Nan, wiping
water from her glasses.

'I did!' said Rosa, happily. Her teeth were chattering a little, but that didn't bother her – she felt as excited and free as the otters.

Rosa lay on her back in a star shape, watching the white clouds drift in the sky, and before she knew it the sea otters and Nan joined in. They all gripped paws, taking hold of Rosa and Nan's hands, and together they floated like an island of fluffy happiness.

'There's nothing like it, is there?' said Oki.

'What say you, my girl?' said Nan.

Rosa didn't need long to come to a decision.

'Nothing like it at all,' she said.

She didn't care that the swimsuit was

tatty and old, and far too big for her. In that short moment, she felt truly a part of nature, truly a part of Big Sky Mountain, and it was wonderful.

13

A Light in the Dark

It was a slow journey back to the cabin with Mr Hibberdee in tow, and although Nan spent much of the time hurrying him along, he was happier than ever with a massive box full of seaweed delights. His trip had been a success after all, and Rosa felt the same, especially as she'd made so many new friends.

Once they'd unpacked and put on

the kettle, Rosa returned to working on the broken radio in the waning light of evening. She felt more confident now, twisting wires and fixing the simple electrics. When a continuous buzz and crackle leapt out of the tiny speaker she felt truly excited. Though she didn't know what to do with it now.

'Blow my trumpet!' cheered Nan, walking out of the cabin to join her with a cup of tea in one hand. 'You've only gone and fixed it, my girl! What have we got to listen to, then?'

Nan turned the tuning knob, attempting to find a radio station. Rosa hadn't used an old-fashioned radio before, and was surprised to hear a lot of different buzzes and crackles and not much else.

'Is that all you get?' she asked. 'Angry noise?'

'No, no,' said Nan. 'There must still be a channel out there somewhere. Wait . . .'

Suddenly a voice broke through the noise. It was a man's voice, and he was reading about the rain and wind.

'It's still there!' cried Nan.

'The weather forecast?' said Rosa.

'My favourite!' she said, happily.

'I was hoping for some music,' said Rosa.

But Nan didn't hear her. She was too busy listening to a weather report about a storm blowing in later that night.

'I can't believe it still works, after all these years!' said Nan, skipping back into the cabin. 'Are you coming in?'

'Not yet,' said Rosa, who was waiting for darkness.

'Well, don't get cold,' said Nan.

'I won't,' said Rosa, and she dropped her hand to her side and stroked Stick, who was lying beside her, exhausted after their long walk.

Mr Hibberdee ambled over.

'What an adventure,' he said, sitting down on a log. He offered Rosa a snack. 'Seaweed crunch? Free of charge?'

Rosa never passed up a free treat, and they sat there chewing in silence as the stars slowly revealed themselves. It didn't take long before Rosa saw what she'd waited and hoped for. A brief, dim flash of light on the horizon to the east.

'The lighthouse!' she said excitedly.

Mr Hibberdee patted her on the back.

'Good job done,' he said, and he popped another seaweed cake into his mouth.

Rosa felt a warm glow inside. Seeing the lighthouse working far away in the distance, she knew that just like Nan had

done all her life, she had made a real
difference on Big Sky Mountain.

It was the best feeling in the world.

Can you find?

Can you help Rosa find these hidden
species on Big Sky Mountain?
They're all somewhere in the book.

Blueberries

Lichen

Great Scallop

Bladderwort

Place a tick under each
box as you find them!

(Answers at the bottom of the page.)

Gorse

Limpet

Sea Kale

Chamomile

Our Oceans

Our oceans are incredibly important to the health of the planet, yet every day we pollute them with plastic.

Rubbish often litters our beaches, but there are also giant patches of plastic waste far out at sea. The largest is the Great Pacific Garbage Patch and is estimated to be three times the size of France! Fish and other sea creatures can mistake plastic bags for food, or get trapped in scraps of netting.

Hermit crabs have really been seen using discarded plastic pipes and waste for shells!

The simplest thing we can do to help keep the seas healthy is to always throw rubbish into a bin or take it home after a trip to the seaside.